A Week With My Aunt

written by Pam Holden
illustrated by Kelvin Hawley

I went to stay with my Aunt for a week.
We had fun every day.

We played games and
we made things.
We went to lots of places.

Monday was a hot day,
so we went to the beach.

4

We had a swim in the sea. Then we caught three fish to take home.

It was windy on Tuesday,
so we went to the park.

We flew our kites high in the sky.
Then we had a picnic lunch.

Wednesday was a cloudy day, so we played outside.

We made a tent in a big tree. Then we picked some flowers and fruit and vegetables.

It was sunny on Thursday,
so we went to the playground.

We went on the seesaw and the merry-go-round. The slide was fun, too.

On Friday, it was a cold day, so we walked in the woods.

We took some pictures of the birds and butterflies. We saw some rabbits, too.

Saturday was a rainy day, so we went to the library.

We listened to some stories.
Then we got three books
to take home.

It was stormy on Sunday, so we played games at home. Then we read our books and we had a rest.